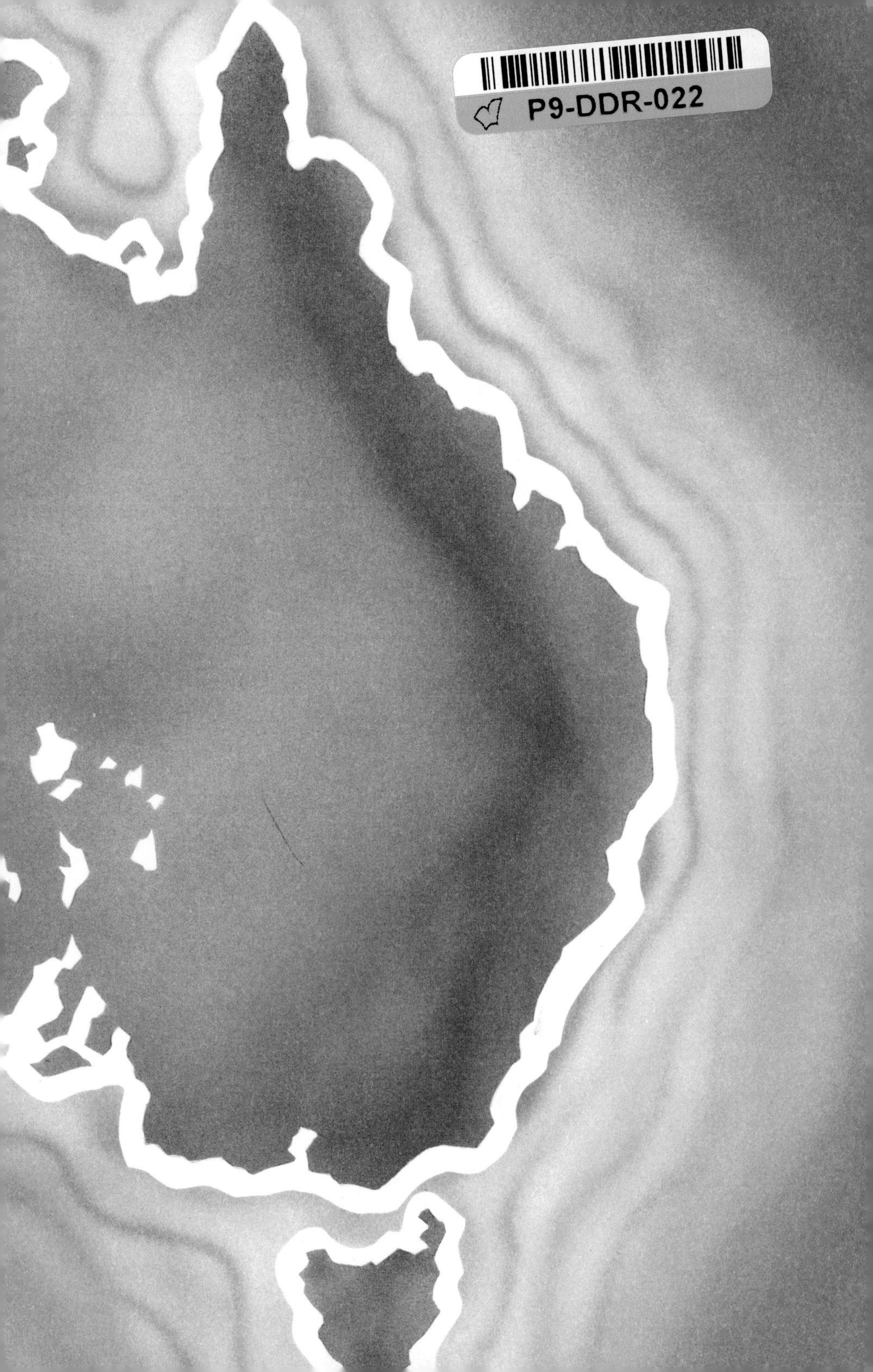

 Published in the United States by Grolier Enterprises Inc., Danbury, Connecticut. Originally published in Denmark as Bernard og Bianca S.O.S. fra Australien by Gutenberghus Gruppen, Copenhagen, in 1991. ISBN: 0-7172-8321-6

Manufactured in the United States.

A B C D 3 4 5 6

# Disney's
# The Rescuers Down Under

The outback of Australia is an exciting place for a boy to grow up. Little Cody loved to explore the wild and rugged terrain. And to visit all his animal friends. Cody was a special boy. He loved animals so

much that he had learned to talk to them and understand their language.

One day, as Cody was out hiking, his friend, Faloo, the kangaroo, came hopping up to him. Faloo looked very worried indeed.

“Cody, thank heavens it’s you!” said Faloo, as she gasped for breath. “You must come at once and use your clever human hands to help. Climb upon my back for we must hurry!”

And as the boy clung on tightly, the kangaroo began to hop.

And as she hopped,
Faloo explained.
"It is our friend, Marahute, the great golden eagle. She's trapped high up on a cliff, in a poacher's net. You're the only one who can climb up there to free her!"

Soon, they reached the cliff and Cody began to climb.

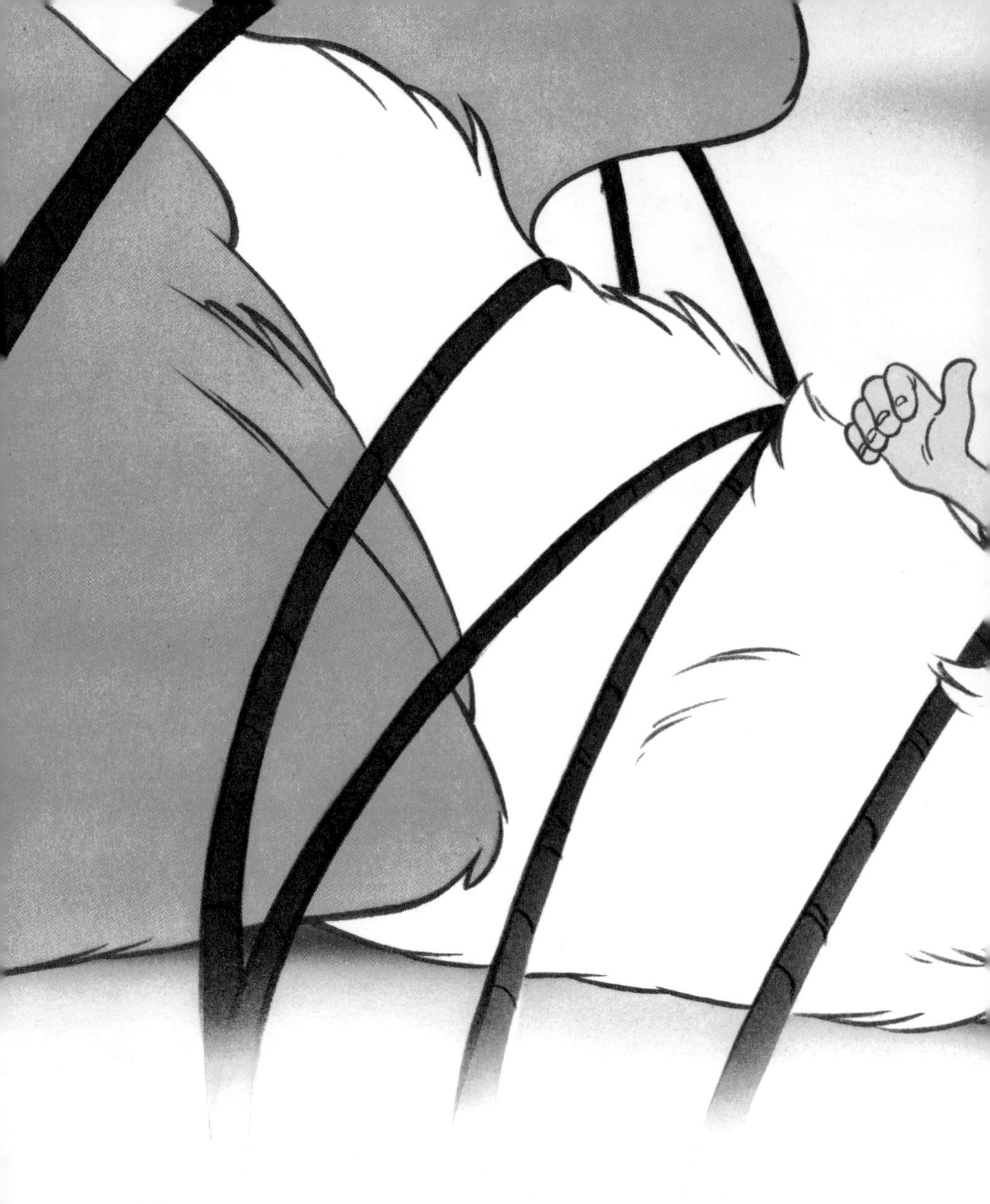

After several minutes, Cody found his old friend, Marahute, bound tight in an evil hunter's trap. When she saw the boy the great eagle ceased her struggling. She smiled and waited patiently for her little friend to free her.

But when the net was loose, Marahute's powerful wing sprang out and accidentally knocked Cody off the ledge.

"Oh, no!" shouted the boy, as he plunged towards the sharp rocks below.

"Help! Save me, Marahute!"

Quickly the giant bird tore herself free from her bonds. She swooped down through the air and caught the boy gently in her talons. He climbed on her back and she carried him across the steep cliffs of the

winding gorges. Back at her nest, she even gave Cody one of her precious feathers, as thanks for saving her from the poacher's clutches.

Later, many miles away, as Cody was walking home, he noticed a little mouse. The mouse was also hopelessly trapped in a poacher's snare. But as Cody bent down to free the little fellow, the mouse shouted, "No, no, you mustn't. You're in great danger!"

It was too late. Cody hadn't seen the deep hole hidden by grass and branches beneath the mouse trap. And down he plunged. As soon as he landed, he heard mocking laughter and he looked up from the hole to see a strange man and a lizard grinning down at him.

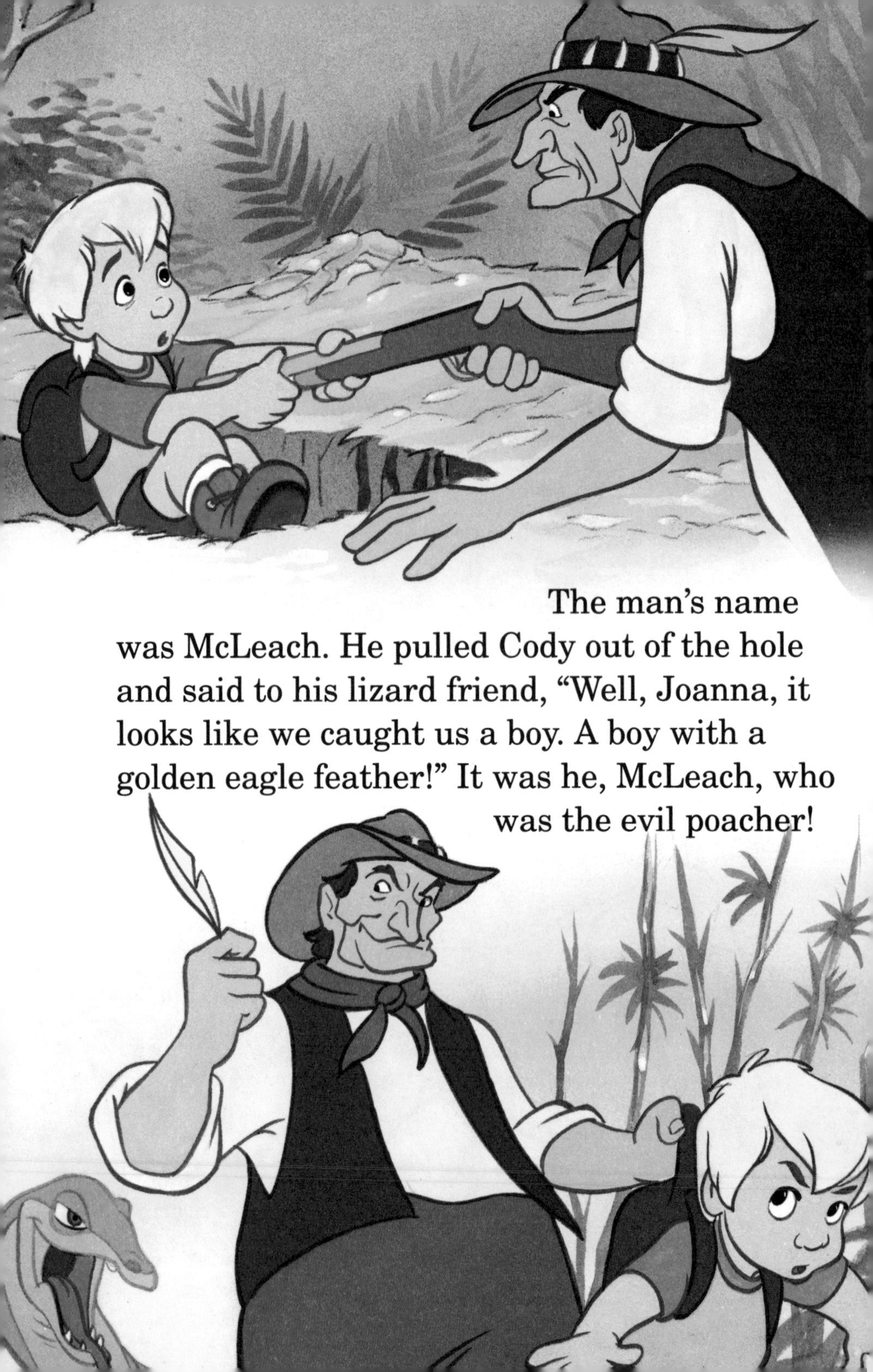

The man's name was McLeach. He pulled Cody out of the hole and said to his lizard friend, "Well, Joanna, it looks like we caught us a boy. A boy with a golden eagle feather!" It was he, McLeach, who was the evil poacher!

Then McLeach took Cody and shoved him roughly into a cage on his horrible poacher's truck. "You're staying there until you tell me where I can find that eagle," he said. "That bird is worth millions to me, boy. Dead or alive!"

The little mouse had been watching. Quickly, he ran to the animal telegraph office so that he could send for help.

A little while later, on the other side of the world, two mice were dining in a restaurant. They were in New York, where it was night, instead of day. Bernard had invited his friend, Bianca, out because he was going to ask her to marry him. But before he could ask her, he dropped the wedding ring and it rolled under the table!

And by the time he came up again, Bianca was reading a note the waiter had brought. "Oh dear, this sounds serious!" she said.

Bianca then told Bernard that they had to rush back to the Rescue Society Headquarters, where they worked. Someone was in trouble. There the two mice learned that a boy named Cody was in great danger in Australia. Because the boy had always helped animals it was Bernard and Bianca's job to go at once and help him.

Unfortunately, the only way of getting to Australia at that time of night was by bird. But what a bird! Wilbur, the albatross, was the oddest fellow they had ever met. "Sure," Wilbur told them, as he laughed and danced around his old house.

"I'll be happy to fly you to Australia. Uh. . . just tell me one thing. What's Australia?"

Soon, Bernard and Bianca were strapped to Wilbur's back, as the big bird fought his way through a snowstorm, following Bianca's directions west. All night and all day he flew, but at last the exhausted albatross reached the sunny shores of the great continent of Australia.

But as Wilbur landed at the Australian headquarters of the Rescue Society, he crashed and sprained a wing. "You'll have to be more careful next time, mate," said Jake, an Australian mouse who was waiting for them.

Because Wilbur had to rest and nurse his injured wing, Jake found another way to fly the mice inland in search of little Cody. "Come on," laughed Jake. "There's nothing like a flight on the back of a good old Australian flying squirrel!"

To his surprise, Bernard soon found out that he missed flying with Wilbur! It was safer!

Meanwhile, in a back room at McLeach's shack, Cody was getting to know some other captives. There was a sad kangaroo named Red, a frustrated koala bear called Krebbs and a frill-necked lizard named Frank, who was trying desperately to escape. After a while, the lizard even tried to use his tail to pick the lock on his cage.

Amazingly, Frank got the lock open.

But how were they to get out of the room? In order to free his friends, the little lizard had to reach a set of keys.

Unluckily, Joanna saw him and chased Frank right back in to his cage.

Meanwhile Bernard, Bianca and Jake, the Australian mouse, were getting closer. The little mouse who had sent the telegram to the Australian section of the Rescue Society, had told Jake just where to search for Cody.

But when Bernard, Bianca and Jake arrived at McLeach's shack, they were surprised to see that the villain was letting the boy go. "I don't need you any more," he told Cody. "I've heard that someone else has just shot your eagle friend dead. So you're no use to me now."

McLeach smiled an evil smile. "It's a shame that eagle's eggs will get cold and die now, with no one to take care of them!" he shouted after the boy.

“Oh, no,” thought Cody, as he hurried towards the cliffs. “I’ve got to save poor Marahute’s eggs!” But it was all a lie. Marahute wasn’t really dead. The cunning McLeach was just trying to trick Cody into showing him where the great eagle lived! And as McLeach followed Cody, the mice leaped unseen aboard the truck to follow McLeach!

When McLeach's truck reached the cliff, the three mice hurried ahead to find Cody. And when they found him at Marahute's nest, Bernard said, "Quick, boy, McLeach has come! And he has plans to capture your eagle friend! We must warn her!" But it was too late. As Marahute returned to the nest, McLeach fired a net right over her!

"Oh, no!" shouted Cody. "This is all my fault! I've got to help her !" And before the mice could

stop him, Cody leaped into the air and caught hold of the net holding the golden eagle.

"Well, well, Joanna," laughed McLeach, as he dropped the net containing the eagle and the boy into the cage on his truck. "It looks like we've caught two foolish birds with one net!"

Then McLeach lowered the big lizard towards Marahute's nest.

"Eat all them eggs now, Joanna," he said. "We want this eagle to be the last one of her kind in the whole world. Then she'll be even more valuable to us when we sell her to a zoo!"

But when the three mice heard this, they quickly hid Marahute's eggs in a crevice and rolled some rocks back into the nest. Rocks that looked just like eggs!

When Joanna reached the nest, she smiled and bit down hard into one ‘egg’. “Ouch!” All she’d managed to do was to crack a tooth. “These eggs must be really hardboiled,” she spluttered. So instead of eating them, she pushed them over the cliff. Meanwhile, Wilbur, the albatross was on his way.

And when the lizard had gone, Wilbur landed near the nest. “Wonderful! Just in time, Wilbur,” smiled Bianca. She came out of hiding and rolled an egg back into the nest. “You’re a nice, big, warm bird. You can sit on these and take care of them.” Wilbur was beginning to feel sorry he had come!

Meanwhile, the evil McLeach decided to lower poor Cody into the river, so the crocodiles could get him.

But brave Bernard hurried back to the truck and shut off the motor to stop McLeach. Still the villainous poacher wasn't beaten. Instead, he broke the rope that held Cody, with a rifle bullet!

And as the poor boy fell into the rushing water, Joanna the lizard chased after Bernard. But clever Bernard ran straight between McLeach's legs and foolish Joanna crashed into the rogue, knocking all three of them into the water.

Once Bernard was in the water, he not only had to try to save Cody from the crocodiles, but from a dangerous waterfall, too! If they were swept over the edge, they would surely be drowned.

But to Bernard and Cody's great relief, they soon heard the beating of great wings and they looked up to see Marahute gliding down to rescue them. Bianca and Jake had succeeded in freeing the great eagle from her cage!

And as Marahute lifted Bernard and Cody into the air, Bernard looked down, just in time to see that rascal, McLeach, and his lizard being swept over the waterfall. It was hard to feel sorry for the two hard-hearted villains.

In no time at all, Cody and his friends, the mice, were high in the air, soaring on the back of the wonderful eagle. Marahute was taking the boy home. And as they flew by her nest, Wilbur the albatross sighed to himself. “I do hope that eagle hurries back,” he said. “If these eggs hatch before she returns. I’m going to end up a mother!”

And as they flew, Bernard finally found the courage to ask Bianca to marry him. “Oh, yes, of course, my hero,” sighed Bianca, as she gave him a big kiss. “I thought you’d never ask!”

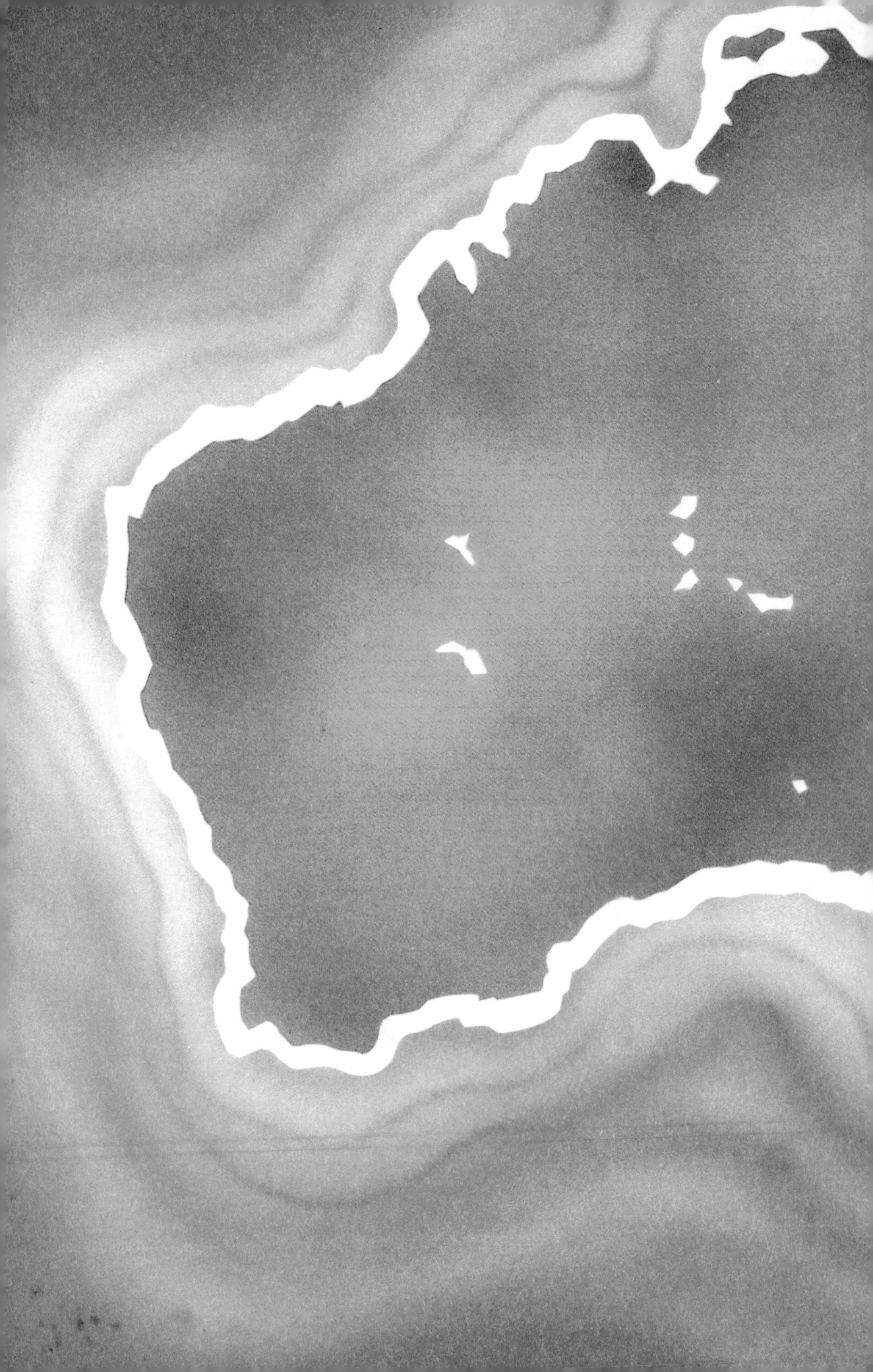